The Beast of Blackwood Forest

The Beast of Blackwood Forest

A HORROR IN THE WILD

Felix Northwood

ECONO Publishing Company

Contents

1

᭟

Chapter 1: Whispering Woods

The sun in the late afternoon filtered through the dense canopy of Blackwood Forest, creating a dappled pattern on the ground covered in fallen leaves. Amelia, an experienced hiker, proceeded cautiously along the narrow and winding trail. Despite hearing the tales and whispered legends about these woods, she dismissed them as mere campfire stories due to her rational mindset. However, as she proceeded further, an inexplicable sensation of coldness ran down her back.

Blackwood Forest is characterized by its ancient trees, which are tall and twisted, with interlocking branches resembling arthritic fingers. As Amelia descended further, she increasingly experienced the overwhelming sense of scrutiny emanating from the forest. The woods appeared animate, with a sense of observation and whispered communication. The atmosphere was filled with the pungent odor of moist soil and decomposing foliage, creating a natural yet disconcerting fragrance.

As daylight diminished, unfamiliar noises permeated the atmosphere. Initially, Amelia attributed the sound to the wind; however, the rhythmic and deliberate nature of the rustling leaves made her doubt this assumption. The conversation was whispered, barely audible, with words that were difficult to understand. She briefly halted, intensifying her auditory focus in an attempt to comprehend the various sounds. Did the whispers become louder and more insistent, or was it just her imagination?

The path meandered, eventually guiding her to a compact clearing. As the sun diminished into a faint glow on the horizon, the surrounding forest appeared to enclose her. As the daylight faded, the trees' elongated and twisted shadows swayed in a haunting manner in response to the wind. Amelia experienced a combination of fear and fascination, causing her heart to race. Despite her initial realization that she should retreat, her curiosity compelled her to continue moving forward.

The clearing contained a centuries-old oak tree with weathered and rugged bark. The whispers appeared to originate from this location, gradually increasing in volume until they formed a collective of subdued voices. Amelia cautiously approached the tree, attentively surveying the dimming forest surroundings. She extended her hand hesitantly towards the coarse bark, sensing an unexplainable attraction to the age-old guardian.

As the woman's fingers made contact with the tree, a strong gust of wind blew across the open space, causing the murmurs to increase in volume and merge into a chaotic blend of unintelligible voices. The temperature dropped and the surrounding environment became filled with an intangible force. Amelia exhaled, creating visible vapor in the cold atmosphere, while experiencing a growing sensation of discomfort.

She retreated from the tree, her eyes displaying a combination of fear and fascination. The whispers suddenly ceased, creating a profound silence. The forest appeared to be in a state of anticipation and observation. Amelia was filled with numerous questions, yet she had an innate understanding that she was not currently destined to discover the answers.

She quickly glanced at the ancient oak before swiftly returning along the path. As she approached the forest's edge, the oppressive atmosphere lifted slightly, suggesting a reluctant release. However, upon her emergence into the diminishing daylight, she experienced a sense of detachment, as if a fragment of her being remained entangled within the murmuring depths of Blackwood Forest.

Amelia reflected on her experience in the forest as she returned to civilization. She attempted to rationalize it as a mere illusion caused by the wind. However, a subconscious awareness suggested the presence of an inexplicable and enigmatic force within the depths of Blackwood Forest.

Amelia arrived at her car, parked at the forest's edge, after the sun had fully set. She returned home without speaking, reflecting on the events of the day. Amelia felt a strong attraction to Blackwood Forest after discovering some of its mysteries, and she was determined to return and uncover the truth about the enigmatic woods.

2

Chapter 2: Shadows at Sundown

As evening descended upon Blackwood Forest, the sky was adorned with shades of deep purple and orange. Mark, a renowned local photographer, embarked on a wilderness expedition to capture the captivating allure of the forest during sunset. Despite hearing stories and whispers about something sinister in the woods, Mark's skepticism outweighed his superstitions.

The forest underwent a significant transformation during dusk. The previously lush vegetation now assumed a more somber and foreboding hue. Mark photographed the interplay of light and shadow created by the setting sun filtering through twisted branches, casting elongated shadows on the forest floor.

As he proceeded further, the illumination diminished, and the shadows extended, resembling elongated dark appendages on the ground. The ambient sounds of the forest, such as the movement of animals and the singing of birds, gradually diminished, giving way to a deep silence that enveloped all other sounds.

Mark briefly halted, experiencing heightened sensory perception. He experienced a disconcerting feeling of being under observation. As the temperature dropped, a gentle mist emerged from the ground, meandering through the forest like ethereal wisps. He observed through his camera lens, in search of an ideal photograph, yet what he witnessed caused him to hesitate.

In the viewfinder, the shadows exhibited autonomous movement, distinct from the diminishing illumination. Initially, there was a subtle and gentle undulating motion, but upon observation, the shadows appeared to increase in both size and intensity. Mark lowered his camera, perplexed by the possibility of his eyes deceiving him.

He decided to leave because the diminishing light posed too much of a risk to proceed. While retracing his path, he was suddenly alerted by a rustling noise. A faint, rustling sound emerged from the area behind the individual, resembling the movement of an object being dragged along the ground in the forest.

Mark experienced an increased heart rate. He swiftly rotated, holding his camera in a defensive posture, yet observed only the thick foliage and the progressively lengthening shadows. He increased his speed, yet the sound of rustling persisted, matching his pace and remaining constantly hidden.

The forest appeared labyrinthine, with the well-known trail becoming convoluted and perplexing due to the limited illumination. Mark's rational thinking led him to believe that the creature he encountered was simply an animal, possibly a deer or a fox. However, a more instinctual fear within him suggested the presence of something much more malevolent.

The shadows enveloped him, transforming the previously recognizable trees into twisted, intimidating forms. Mark's respiration was rapid and shallow. From his vantage point, he observed the forest's periphery in the far distance, where the diminishing sunlight faintly illuminated the path ahead.

Abruptly, he tripped on a protruding root, resulting in a forceful impact with the ground. The camera was accidentally dropped and landed a short distance away. As he quickly rose, a looming and formidable shadow cast itself over him. Mark's body became immobile, and his eyes widened in a state of extreme fear.

Briefly, he perceived a dark figure, appearing as a silhouette amidst the surrounding shadows. However, as he blinked, the entity vanished, blending seamlessly into the obscurity. Mark acted without hesitation. He quickly grabbed his camera and fled.

The air was filled with the sounds of his heavy footsteps and labored breathing as he emerged from the forest and reached the safety of the open field. He continued running until he arrived at his car, which was parked on the outskirts of the forest.

Breathless, he propped himself against the vehicle, his thoughts in a flurry. What was his observation? Did the shadows appear to come alive due to an optical illusion or was it an actual occurrence? Mark's familiarity with the forest did not prepare him for the inexplicable events he encountered tonight.

He briefly looked back at the forest, which was now enveloped in darkness at its periphery. The sensation of being observed had diminished, yet a sense of discomfort remained. Mark was hesitant to examine his photos due to his fear of discovering unsettling images that the camera might have captured during sunset.

He took a deep breath, entered his vehicle, and departed, leaving the enigma of Blackwood Forest in his wake. However, as he checked the rearview mirror, he couldn't shake the unsettling sensation that an unseen presence from the forest was observing him as he departed, concealed within the shadows during dusk.

3

Chapter 3: The Unseen Stalker

The night in Blackwood Forest was exceptionally calm. Julia, a wildlife biologist, established her camp in a small clearing, enclosed by the dense and tall forest trees. The individual's primary objective was to conduct research on nocturnal animals. However, on this particular evening, their concentration was interrupted by an unsettling sensation of being under observation.

The campfire emitted crackling and popping sounds, creating a warm glow in the vicinity of her tent. Julia recorded her observations while sitting on a fallen log, holding her notebook. The typical sounds of the forest, such as owl hoots and small creature rustling, appeared subdued tonight, suggesting a sense of anticipation in the forest.

While taking notes, Julia felt a persistent sense of being observed. The sensation was instinctual, evoking a bodily response characterized by raised hairs on the nape. She gazed into the darkness outside the range of the fire, her eyes attempting to penetrate the complete absence of light. However, all she observed was the profound and impenetrable darkness within the forest.

Julia, having made the decision to retire early, took the necessary steps to secure her food supplies and extinguish the fire. She entered her tent, finding little solace in the fabric walls amidst the expansive forest surroundings. As she rested in her sleeping bag, the sensation of being observed grew stronger.

Julia experienced insomnia as time elapsed. The silence of the night heightened the perception of even the slightest sounds. Suddenly, she detected a faint, almost imperceptible noise resembling the gentle tread of footsteps on the ground of the forest. She experienced a momentary cardiac irregularity. She remained motionless, attentively listening.

The footsteps appeared to move in a deliberate and measured manner around the tent. Julia's mind was filled with various possibilities. Was the creature in question merely inquisitive, or did it possess a more malevolent nature? She recalled the folklore surrounding Blackwood Forest, which consisted of stories about a mysterious creature that hunted unsuspecting travelers. Previously disregarded as mere myths, her skepticism wavered as doubt infiltrated her thoughts amidst the obscurity of the forest.

The footsteps ceased suddenly, and were followed by a deep, throaty growl originating just outside her tent. Julia experienced a sudden interruption in her breathing. She hesitated before reaching for her flashlight. Was her desire to explore her surroundings genuine?

With a surge of bravery, Julia cautiously unzipped the tent flap to take a quick glimpse of the outside. The flashlight beam penetrated the darkness, illuminating only the presence of trees and shadows. The growling had stopped, and the forest was now unnervingly quiet.

Abruptly, the observer's attention was drawn to a swift and unidentified shadow moving amongst the trees. Julia experienced an increased heart rate. She closed the tent flap quickly, feeling overwhelmed. What entity or presence was pursuing her within the obscurity?

She remained awake for an extended period, perceiving the passage of time as hours, with each sound eliciting a surge of apprehension. She eventually succumbed to exhaustion and entered a restless sleep, haunted by dreams of mysterious figures and unseen gazes.

The morning arrived with the gentle illumination of dawn. Julia emerged from her tent, surveying the clearing. In the daylight, the forest appeared ordinary, with its previously foreboding atmosphere replaced by the tranquility inherent in the natural environment. However, the ground presented a contrasting narrative.

Unfamiliar tracks surrounded the vicinity of her tent, differing from any known animal species. The objects exhibited significant size and irregularity, closely resembling the form of a humanoid. Julia experienced cognitive difficulty in comprehending the situation. The tracks encircled the tent and subsequently vanished into the forest, suggesting the sudden disappearance of the entity responsible for their creation.

Julia concluded her stay in Blackwood Forest and commenced the process of dismantling her camp. While her scientific inclination urged her to remain and conduct further investigation, her instincts compelled her to retreat from the unknown presence concealed within the forest.

While returning to her vehicle, Julia couldn't resist the urge to periodically look behind her, anticipating the presence of a pursuer. However, the surroundings were devoid of any significant auditory stimuli, except for the gentle rustling of leaves and the typical ambient noises commonly associated with a forest environment.

The encounter in Blackwood Forest would remain with her, serving as a poignant reminder that certain enigmas are better left unresolved. Julia was haunted by an unseen presence that emanated from the depths of the forest, an experience she believed she would always remember.

4

∽

Chapter 4: Midnight Howls

In the center of Blackwood Forest, the night had descended, enveloping everything in an aura of enigma. Ethan, an individual known for exploring local legends, established his camp in a remote area of the forest with the intention of investigating the veracity of the unsettling stories associated with this particular woodland. He was fascinated by accounts of peculiar midnight howls that reverberated through the trees, possessing an ethereal nature.

The equipment he possessed consisted of a recorder for sound capture, a night-vision camera, and a keen sense of curiosity that had led him into numerous adventures. As midnight approached, Ethan sat by his fire, listening to the sounds of the forest at night.

The typical nocturnal sounds were present, including the chirping of crickets and the sporadic hooting of an owl. As midnight neared, a noticeable transformation occurred in the forest. The temperature dropped, the wind stopped rustling the leaves, and a profound stillness settled over the forest.

Ethan verified the readiness of his recorder for sound capture. The level of anticipation was nearly intolerable. At the stroke of midnight, a melancholic howl emerged from the depths of the forest.

The sound possessed a haunting quality, evoking a sense of sorrow and longing that deeply affected Ethan emotionally. He quickly retrieved his recorder and raised it to record the sound. The melancholic howl echoed through the ancient trees, evoking a sense of longing for something or someone lost in the depths of history.

Ethan rose in response to the sound of the howl. He had to locate the source. Armed with a flashlight and a running recorder, he ventured into the darkness, pursuing a sound that elusively traversed the forest.

The persistent howls guided him further into the forest. The terrain became more rugged and the underbrush denser. Ethan experienced a combination of fear and excitement, causing his heart to race. The sound was in close proximity, nearly directly overhead.

He glanced upwards, illuminating the surrounding darkness with his flashlight, and observed a silhouette positioned atop an elevated branch. Initially, the observer perceived the object as a sizable avian creature. However, upon closer examination, he discerned that it did not possess the characteristics of a bird. The size and humanoid appearance of the figure were excessive.

The figure appeared to be the origin of the howls, but it was unfamiliar to Ethan in terms of its appearance and knowledge. The object was concealed in darkness, making its characteristics indistinguishable, except for its faintly glowing eyes that displayed a profound and perceptive intellect in the flashlight's illumination.

Ethan experienced a rapid flow of thoughts. Could this be the creature responsible for the legends? The guardian of Blackwood Forest, characterized by its mournful howls that conveyed ancient secrets and concealed truths.

Ethan was captivated as he witnessed the figure emit a profound, prolonged howl that reverberated throughout the forest, profoundly affecting his inner being. Subsequently, with a smooth and ethereal motion, it sprang from the tree and vanished into the darkness.

The forest gradually regenerated, with the nocturnal sounds resuming their harmonious chorus. Ethan remained motionless, holding his recorder, attempting to comprehend the recent event he had observed. The howling had stopped, resulting in a deep silence.

He returned to his camp, his mind filled with a flurry of thoughts and inquiries. The encounter was short but had a lasting impact on him. The midnight howls and presence of a mysterious figure in the trees presented a perplexing and intriguing puzzle, inviting investigation and resolution.

Ethan was compelled to revisit Blackwood Forest due to its enigmatic nature and the eerie midnight howls. However, at present, he possessed a recording that required analysis, serving as evidence of an extraordinary occurrence that remained inexplicable.

At daybreak, Ethan sat near the fading flames of his fire, listening to the recorder replaying the eerie howls. The protagonist was aware of the profound and enigmatic secrets concealed within Blackwood Forest, surpassing his previous expectations. He possessed a resolute determination to unveil these secrets, regardless of the challenges he might encounter.

5

Chapter 5: The Forgotten Trail

At dawn, the sunlight started to filter through the thick foliage of Blackwood Forest, creating a golden glow that illuminated the mist enveloping the trees. Sarah, an enthusiastic adventurer with a passion for local legends, set out on a mission to locate the Forgotten Trail, a rumored path shrouded in enigma and forgotten over the years.

Equipped with a discovered antiquated map from the local historical archives, Sarah embarked on a journey into the central region of the forest. The map, although worn and faded with frayed edges, represented the closest lead to the trail that has been discovered in several decades.

The early morning forest was characterized by tranquility and dimness. Sarah proceeded cautiously, her gaze meticulously surveying the vegetation, diligently seeking any indication of the path. Based on the map, the route was in close proximity to Weaver's Creek, a stream known for its clear and cold water, even during the summer months.

As Sarah approached the creek, she was guided by the sound of running water and observed something unusual. The surrounding vegetation appeared less dense, with slightly greater spacing between the trees. Although not immediately noticeable, a trained observer would recognize the subtle indications of a path that has been reclaimed by nature over a significant period of time.

The Forgotten Trail initially appeared as a mere opening in the vegetation, as indicated by the map. Sarah eagerly made her way through the crowd, her enthusiasm intensifying with each stride. The trail was barely visible due to overgrowth, yet it remained discernible. She traversed a rarely trodden path, which had been devoid of footprints for an extended period of time.

As she continued her exploration, the forest underwent noticeable transformations. The trees in this location exhibited signs of age, characterized by thick and gnarled trunks and twisted branches that assumed peculiar, almost unnatural forms. The temperature of the air dropped and the lighting became more subdued, suggesting that the forest was cognizant of her presence in its secluded domain.

Sarah observed unusual markings on several trees, which appeared to be ancient carvings resembling symbols or signs. The weathered and indecipherable markings seemed to indicate the trail, leading her further into the forest. She pondered the origins of the hands responsible for their creation, contemplating the narratives and hidden knowledge they possessed.

The trail led the individual to a clearing where sunlight penetrated the overhead foliage, illuminating an aged stone structure situated at the focal point. The altar, small and rudimentary, was adorned with moss and lichen, its purpose obscured by the passage of time.

Sarah nervously approached the altar, experiencing a combination of apprehension and intrigue. The surrounding air was filled with the aroma of soil and aged rock. The altar displayed a deliberate arrangement of stones, feathers, and what seemed to be bones.

She extended her hand to make contact with one of the stones, gently running her fingers along its cool and polished exterior. As she experienced the sensation, a shiver traveled down her spinal column. The surrounding forest appeared to be in a state of complete silence, as if it was holding its breath.

Suddenly, a melancholic howl emerged from the depths of the forest, disrupting the tranquility. Its resonance appeared to connect with the stones of the altar. Sarah's eyes widened with a sense of alarm. The sound was haunting and evoked a palpable sense of sorrow.

She retreated from the altar, her thoughts in a state of rapid movement. The protagonist followed the Forgotten Trail to a concealed secret located within the depths of Blackwood Forest. However, the howl served as a reminder that certain secrets may be intended to remain concealed, protected by the forest and its unseen residents.

Sarah glanced at the altar and clearing before retracing her steps along the trail. As she departed, the forest appeared observant, with the trees murmuring amongst each other and the lingering echo of a howl resonating in her ears.

Upon exiting the forest, the sunlight appeared more intense, illuminating the external world with enhanced clarity. Sarah was aware that she had encountered a remarkable event, a brief insight into the essence of Blackwood Forest and its overlooked history.

However, the haunting howl served as a constant reminder of the enigmatic nature of the forest, particularly the Forgotten Trail and its concealed secrets.

6

✦

Chapter 6: Eyes in the Darkness

The moon illuminated Blackwood Forest, creating a haunting atmosphere with its silver glow and casting shadows amidst the thick trees. Alex, an experienced photographer with a particular interest in the mysterious allure of the night, had entered the forest to capture its essence during nighttime. The individual had consistently discovered tranquility in engaging in night photography. However, on this particular occasion, the forest appeared to possess a distinct aura, evoking a heightened sense of vitality, as if concealing enigmatic truths within its dimly lit recesses.

While setting up his tripod, Alex observed something peculiar as his camera was directed towards a remarkably twisted and aged tree. The atmosphere surrounding him appeared to become denser, infused with an inexplicable force. The forest became eerily quiet, with the usual sounds of nocturnal animals abruptly ceasing.

He observed the scene through the viewfinder of his camera,

making necessary adjustments to the focus. He noticed pairs of luminous eyes, small yet clearly discernible, observing him from the shadows. Surprised, he quickly lowered his camera and scanned the surrounding forest. Numerous eyes were concealed amidst the trees, attentively observing him.

Alex experienced an increased heart rate. He possessed knowledge of the fauna in Blackwood Forest, however, the current situation presented a distinct contrast. The eyes were unidentifiable to him as belonging to any known animal. The presence of a large number of individuals was excessive and characterized by heightened vigilance. He experienced a shiver of fear upon realizing his solitude had been disrupted.

Feeling increasingly unsettled, he made the decision to gather his belongings. As he performed the action, the eyes attentively tracked his movements without blinking or diverting their gaze. The reflective spots in the dark emitted a tangible presence, suggesting intelligence and purpose.

Alex hastened his speed, eager to depart from the forest and evade its vigilant gaze. While walking, he observed that the eyes appeared to follow his movements, maintaining synchrony in the absence of light. They remained at a distance, yet consistently present, lingering on the periphery of the illumination provided by his flashlight.

He was overwhelmed with various potential outcomes. Might these beings correspond to the mythical creatures he had been informed of, the protectors of the woodland, or perhaps something of a supernatural nature? He had arrived in search of the nocturnal aesthetics, but instead encountered the enigmatic aspects of the night.

Alex glanced back one final time as he approached the forest's edge. The eyes remained, observing his departure. He experienced a complex blend of emotions, including both relief and disappointment. He felt torn between the desire to stay and uncover the truth behind the enigmatic gaze, and the inclination to depart and evade the disconcerting scrutiny of the unseen observers.

Upon exiting the forest, the protagonist experienced a perceptible shift in the atmosphere, characterized by a sense of weightlessness and a departure from the previous realm. He returned home with the vivid memory of glowing eyes, serving as a haunting reminder of the mysterious presence that resides in the darkness of Blackwood Forest.

That evening, while lying in bed, Alex's mind was filled with a multitude of thoughts. The enigmatic eyes concealed within the shadows tested his understanding of the natural realm, alluding to undiscovered secrets. He was aware that he would revisit Blackwood Forest due to its mysterious nature and the presence of enigmatic beings lurking in its shadows.

Currently, he found satisfaction in the photographs he had captured, each one depicting the captivating allure of the nocturnal forest. In each photograph, one could discern minuscule specks of light in the background, scarcely perceptible. These faint illuminations serve as a silent testament to the unseen observers who watched him in the shadows.

7

Chapter 7: The Haunting of Hollow's Creek

Blackwood Forest was enveloped in a somber atmosphere due to the presence of low-hanging clouds on an overcast day. Emily, a young writer with a strong interest in the supernatural, visited Hollow's Creek, a location known for its unsettling ambiance and haunted folklore. The individual aimed to collect material for her upcoming novel, yet as she proceeded further into the forest, she experienced a slight sense of unease.

According to local folklore, Hollow's Creek is believed to be haunted by the spirits of individuals who perished in the surrounding forest. Their ethereal voices are said to be carried by the wind, while their profound grief is believed to be ingrained in the creek bed's stones. As Emily neared the creek, she noticed a significant drop in temperature, which sharply contrasted with the otherwise mild autumn weather.

The creek was a slender and winding watercourse, characterized by its calm and opaque waters. The surrounding trees exhibited an inward inclination, with their branches interweaving to form a dense overhead canopy. Emily experienced a sense of entering an alternate realm, a location unaffected by the passage of time.

She arranged her recording equipment in anticipation of capturing any atypical sounds or whispers. The creek was characterized by a profound and almost oppressive silence. Emily perched on a rock, attentively absorbing the surroundings, her senses attuned to any potential signs of the supernatural.

As she sat, she perceived a sound that started off faint but gradually increased in volume. The sound of voices emanated from the creek, resembling whispers and murmurs. The voices were unclear, yet their tone conveyed a mournful sentiment, characterized by a profound longing and sadness that deeply affected her.

Emily's hands trembled as she reached for her recorder. She had sought this outcome, yet as it unfolded, she experienced a sudden wave of apprehension. The indistinct whispers appeared to be addressing her directly, their meaning just beyond comprehension.

As she listened, a mist started to emerge from the creek, enveloping her. The temperature decreased, causing Emily to observe her breath becoming visible in the frigid air. She experienced a sensation of a presence, an intangible force that appeared to surround her.

Subsequently, she observed the emergence of faint and ethereal figures from the mist, their forms resembling mere shadows. They exhibited a deliberate and graceful movement, characterized by a slow pace. Their gaze appeared vacant, yet focused on her.

Emily experienced an increased heart rate. Despite her desire to flee, she found herself immobilized, unable to make her legs propel her forward. She was captivated by the apparitions, attempting to comprehend the phenomenon she was observing. The approaching figures closed in, their whispers increasing in volume, until they surrounded her.

Subsequently, the entities disappeared abruptly, causing the mist to disperse simultaneously. The whispering stopped, leaving only the gentle sound of the creek flowing over the rocks.

Emily remained in a state of shock, clutching her recorder. She had arrived with the intention of encountering spirits, and she had successfully done so. However, the actual experience did not align with her initial expectations. The experience evoked strong emotions of fear and deep sorrow, providing insight into a realm inhabited by individuals yearning for eternity.

Emily realized that her novel would be permanently altered by her experiences at Hollow's Creek as she packed up her equipment. The haunting surpassed her expectations in terms of its reality.

Upon departing Hollow's Creek, she experienced a profound sense of wonder and developed a profound reverence for the enigmatic aspects of Blackwood Forest. The haunting of Hollow's Creek served as a tangible reminder of the blurred boundary between the living and the deceased, transcending mere folklore and becoming a palpable reality.

8

~

Chapter 8: Secrets under the Moonlight

The full moon illuminated Blackwood Forest, casting a silver glow and turning the dense woods into a realm of enchanting beauty. Thomas, a local historian with a profound fascination for the enigmatic narratives of the forest, embarked on a nocturnal expedition to unravel a long-standing mystery that had engrossed him over the course of several years.

He intended to reach a secluded and obscure clearing located deep within the forest, which was familiar to only a select few individuals. According to legend, the clearing was believed to be a location where ancient rituals and concealed secrets were unveiled solely during the illumination of a full moon.

Thomas confidently traversed the forest, occasionally using his flashlight to scan the underbrush, but primarily relying on the moon's natural light. The night resounded with the noises of nocturnal animals, forming a symphony that accompanied him during his journey.

After one hour of hiking, he reached the clearing. The location was tranquil, with a grassy ground surrounded by a circle of ancient, twisted trees. At the clearing's center, a solitary stone, aged and adorned with moss, displayed inscriptions of ancient symbols.

Thomas positioned his camera to record the scene, where the moonlight created elongated and striking shadows on the open space. He subsequently retrieved his notes and proceeded to compare the symbols inscribed on the stone with those documented in his research. Every symbol represented a fragment of a larger puzzle, an engraved narrative eagerly awaiting narration.

Thomas observed an anomaly while examining the symbols. The moonlight appeared to interact with the stone, resulting in a subtle luminescence of the symbols. Curious, he approached, feeling a surge of excitement as he neared his newfound revelation.

The symbols, now illuminated, portrayed ancient rituals with people congregating under the moon, raising their arms in celebration or supplication. Thomas recognized the historical and spiritual significance of his current location.

Deeply engrossed in his observations, the observer nearly overlooked the faint rustling sound emanating from behind him. He observed a figure emerging from the edge of the forest. The individual was an elderly man with a weathered face resembling stone, and his eyes reflected the moonlight.

Thomas greeted the old man cautiously, however, the old man only nodded, his attention focused on the radiant stone. He commenced speaking with a hushed yet distinct voice, which resonated in the tranquility of the nocturnal ambiance.

The elderly man informed Thomas about the historical background of the clearing, including the previous inhabitants of the surrounding forest, their cultural beliefs, and the rituals they performed during full moon nights. He discussed the profound bond they had with the forest, the undisclosed knowledge they had protected, and the enduring heritage they had bequeathed.

Thomas attentively listened, recording every word with his recorder. The elderly man's narrative intricately intertwined historical and mythical elements, effectively connecting the past with the present. He discussed the forest's inclination to safeguard its mysteries, divulging them solely to individuals who genuinely endeavored to comprehend.

Upon the conclusion of the old man's narrative, the initial rays of daybreak gradually infiltrated the atmosphere, causing the symbols inscribed on the stone to gradually diminish in visibility. The elderly man silently retreated into the forest, just as he had arrived.

Thomas found himself alone in the clearing, experiencing a surreal sensation reminiscent of a dream. The recording and photos in his possession served as evidence of the events that transpired during the night.

Upon departing from the clearing, he experienced a deep feeling of appreciation and obligation. The artifacts hidden under the moonlight were not merely historical objects, but rather a testament to a neglected culture and a link to the land that remains significant in the present, just as it was in the past.

As Thomas returned through the awakening forest, with the early morning sunlight seeping through the trees, he realized that his perception of Blackwood Forest had been permanently altered. The location possessed not only aesthetic appeal, but also served as a repository of narratives and protector of undisclosed information that only became apparent during nighttime.

9

Chapter 9: The Curse of Old Birch

The morning mist enveloped Blackwood Forest, obscuring its trails with an ethereal cover. Laura, an anthropologist specializing in local folklore, arrived to study the legend of the Old Birch, a tree that is reputedly cursed and feared by the community.

The Old Birch tree, as depicted in folklore, served as a gathering spot for witches and was associated with malevolent sorcery and ill fate. Individuals who had the audacity to harm or make contact with the tree were believed to experience peculiar and unfortunate outcomes.

Laura's forest journey was characterized by tranquility, with only the sound of her footsteps and sporadic avian calls in the distance. The author observed that the wildlife in this area of the woods also avoided it, contributing to the unsettling ambiance.

Eventually, she reached the location of the Old Birch. In a small clearing, a solitary tree stood with pale bark and contorted branches resembling skeletal fingers. Laura experienced a chilling sensation as she approached, despite her initial skepticism.

The observer conducted a thorough examination of the tree, paying close attention to its dimensions and the distinctive markings on its bark. The antiquity of the object was evident, and its potential to evoke superstition was apparent to her. The atmosphere surrounding the Old Birch exhibited a lower temperature, and the mist exhibited a tendency to persist in this location, displaying a reluctance to disperse despite the progression of the morning.

While circling the tree, Laura noticed a set of carvings on the bark. Despite their age and wear, the symbols and figures remained distinguishable, suggesting a narrative. Intrigued by their potential significance, she used her camera to document them.

As she focused on her task, a sudden gust of wind caused the leaves of the Old Birch tree to rustle, creating a whisper-like sound. The temperature decreased, and Laura experienced an inexplicable sensation of being observed.

Subsequently, she perceived a melodious and gentle voice emanating from the vicinity of the tree. Laura glanced around, but there was no visible presence. The voice persisted, conveying a sense of urgency despite its unclear words.

Laura approached the Old Birch with a mixture of fear and intrigue. The volume of the voice increased, allowing her to discern words spoken in an ancient dialect. The text described a bygone era characterized by ceremonies and commitments made beneath the moonlit heavens.

Laura's skepticism diminished as she listened. The legend of the Old Birch holds significance beyond a mere story, as it represents a historical artifact embodying forgotten beliefs and practices.

As she pondered upon this disclosure, the voice diminished and the wind subsided. The temperature reverted to its usual state, leading to the dissipation of the mist. Laura pondered, her preconceived beliefs about folklore being questioned by the encounter.

After her departure from the clearing, she gained a heightened appreciation for the folklore surrounding Blackwood Forest. The realization dawned upon her that the Curse of Old Birch held significance beyond its role as a mere cautionary tale for children. It served as a testament to the deeply ingrained beliefs of the people who once coexisted harmoniously with these woods, with their narratives intricately interwoven into the essence of the forest itself.

Laura diligently reviewed her notes and recordings in her office, with a strong determination to further investigate the Old Birch and its significance in the local folklore. The tree, beyond being a cursed relic, served as a conduit to the past, harboring enigmatic secrets that awaited discovery by those courageous enough to heed its call.

10

Chapter 10: Ghostly Echoes

The evening air was crisp as Michael, an audio engineer with a fascination for the supernatural, ventured into Blackwood Forest. Equipped with his high-sensitivity microphones and recording gear, his objective was to capture the so-called 'Ghostly Echoes' that many locals claimed to have heard resonating through the forest at night.

Blackwood Forest, with its dense canopy and ancient trees, had always been a place of mystery and legend. The Ghostly Echoes were a recent addition to the lore, described as haunting sounds that mimicked human voices, yet belonged to no living person.

As night enveloped the forest, Michael set up his equipment in a small clearing. He adjusted his headphones, tuning into the subtle sounds of the forest. The night was alive with the rustling of leaves, the occasional snap of a twig, but nothing out of the ordinary.

Hours passed, and Michael began to wonder if the Ghostly Echoes were merely a product of overactive imaginations. Just as he considered packing up, he heard it—a faint whisper, almost inaudible, drifting through the trees.

He quickly adjusted his equipment, enhancing the sensitivity. The whisper grew clearer, and to his astonishment, it sounded like a voice, a soft, sorrowful voice speaking in a language he couldn't understand.

The voice seemed to come from all around him, echoing off the trees, creating a chorus of ghostly whispers. Michael's heart raced with excitement and a touch of fear. This was what he had come for, but now that he was hearing it, the reality of the situation was overwhelming.

He tried to locate the source of the voice, moving slowly through the clearing, his microphones extended before him. The whispers seemed to move, always just out of reach, a haunting melody that filled the forest.

As he delved deeper into the source of the sound, Michael began to feel a presence, an unseen entity that seemed to be communicating through these echoes. The whispers were not just random sounds; they were deliberate, imbued with emotion and purpose.

Suddenly, the forest fell silent, the whispers ceasing as abruptly as they had begun. Michael stood in the silence, his heart pounding in his chest. He knew he had just experienced something extraordinary.

He returned to his equipment, replaying the recordings. The voices were there, clear and unmistakable. They were indeed ghostly echoes, but their origin and meaning remained a mystery.

Over the following days, Michael analyzed the recordings, trying to decipher the language and the message. He consulted with linguists and historians, but the voice remained a puzzle, its words lost in the annals of time.

The experience in Blackwood Forest changed Michael. He had always been a skeptic, looking for logical explanations for the supernatural. But the Ghostly Echoes defied explanation. They were a phenomenon that blurred the line between the living and the spectral, a haunting reminder of the mysteries that lay hidden in the heart of Blackwood Forest.

Michael continued his work, returning to the forest, hoping to capture more of the Ghostly Echoes. Each visit brought new sounds, new whispers, each one a piece of a puzzle that he was determined to solve.

The Ghostly Echoes of Blackwood Forest remained an enigma, a spectral chorus that whispered of forgotten stories and hidden truths, echoing through the trees, waiting for someone to understand their haunting melody.

11

Chapter 11: The Lost Camper

The dense fog of early morning cloaked Blackwood Forest in a shroud of mystery. Jack, a seasoned park ranger, had received a report of a camper who had gone missing the night before. His task was to find the camper, a task made more daunting by the forest's reputation for disorienting even the most experienced hikers.

Jack embarked on his search at the crack of dawn, armed with a map, compass, and years of experience navigating the treacherous terrain of the forest. The missing camper, a young man named Tyler, was known to have set up camp near Falcon's Peak, a popular but remote area in the heart of Blackwood.

The forest in the early hours had an eerie stillness. The usually vibrant sounds of wildlife were muffled by the fog, creating a sense of isolation. Jack moved methodically, scanning the area, calling out Tyler's name. His voice seemed to be swallowed by the mist, adding to the unsettling atmosphere.

As he trekked deeper into the forest, Jack noticed something unusual—a series of disorganized footprints in the damp soil, leading off the main path. They were fresh, indicating Tyler had wandered off sometime during the night. Jack followed the tracks, his instincts as a ranger kicking in.

The footprints led him through dense underbrush and overgrown trails, areas of the forest seldom visited. The terrain became rougher, the trees closer together, their branches forming a tangled canopy overhead. Jack noted broken twigs and disturbed leaves, signs of someone moving hastily and without direction.

The trail led to a small, secluded clearing. Jack's heart sank as he saw the remains of a campsite, the tent collapsed and supplies scattered. Tyler's backpack lay open, its contents spilled onto the ground. It looked as if he had left in a hurry, or worse, been forced to.

Jack approached the tent, calling out for Tyler. There was no response. He checked inside the tent, finding Tyler's sleeping bag empty, but with his phone and flashlight still inside. It was clear that Tyler had left the campsite unprepared.

The ranger surveyed the area, trying to piece together what had happened. The disarray suggested a struggle or panic, but there were no signs of another person or animal. It was as if the forest itself had caused the chaos.

Jack's search became more desperate. He expanded the perimeter, looking for any further signs of Tyler. Hours passed, the fog slowly lifting, but there was no sign of the young camper. The forest seemed to have swallowed him whole.

As the day wore on, Jack's concern grew. He knew the dangers of Blackwood Forest, especially for those unfamiliar with its deceptive paths and hidden pitfalls. He called in for backup, knowing that time was of the essence.

The search party arrived, and they combed the forest, their calls for Tyler echoing among the trees. But as evening approached, there was still no sign of the lost camper.

Jack refused to give up. He decided to retrace Tyler's steps, looking for any clue he might have missed. As he walked back to the clearing, he noticed something he hadn't seen before—a small, barely visible path leading away from the campsite, hidden by dense foliage.

Following the path, Jack found himself in a part of the forest he hadn't explored before. The trees here were older, their trunks massive and covered in moss. The air was cooler, the atmosphere heavier. Jack felt a sense of foreboding, but he pushed forward.

Finally, as the light began to fade, Jack heard a faint sound—a voice, weak and trembling. He rushed towards it, calling out Tyler's name. Through a thick cluster of bushes, he found Tyler, injured and disoriented, but alive.

Tyler had fallen into a hidden ravine, twisting his ankle. Disoriented and in pain, he had been unable to find his way back. He had survived the cold night by huddling under leaves and branches.

Jack administered first aid and called for an evacuation team. As they waited, Tyler spoke of his ordeal, of how the forest had seemed to change around him, the paths twisting and turning, leading him further astray. It was as if the forest had a mind of its own, a malevolent force that disoriented and misled.

As the rescue team arrived and Tyler was carried to safety, Jack couldn't help but wonder about the mysterious forces at play in Blackwood Forest. The lost camper had been found, but the secrets of the forest remained, hidden in the mist and the shadows of the ancient trees.

12

Chapter 12: Blood on the Bark

The morning light filtered weakly through the dense canopy of Blackwood Forest, doing little to dispel the chill in the air. Detective Mara Stevens stepped carefully along the rugged path, her eyes scanning the underbrush. She had been called to the forest to investigate a disturbing find - a series of trees marked with what appeared to be blood.

Mara, known for her sharp investigative skills and no-nonsense approach, had seen her share of unusual cases, but this was different. The forest had an unsettling reputation, and the sight of the bloodied trees only added to the sense of dread that hung over the area.

As she approached the first marked tree, she noted the eerie silence of the forest. The usual sounds of wildlife were conspicuously absent, as if the creatures of the forest were holding their breath. The tree in question stood like a silent sentinel, its bark marred by dark red streaks that stood out starkly against the white bark.

Mara donned her gloves and carefully examined the markings. The blood was fresh, not more than a few hours old. It was smeared in a way that suggested a struggle, or perhaps a message, though its meaning was unclear.

She took samples of the blood, her mind racing through the possibilities. Animal attack? A ritualistic act? Or something even more sinister? The forest held its secrets tightly.

The detective moved deeper into the forest, following a trail of bloodied trees. Each one was marked similarly, the red stains a stark contrast to the surrounding greenery. The pattern seemed random, but Mara knew better than to dismiss any detail in a case like this.

As she progressed, the forest seemed to close in around her. The trees grew denser, their branches intertwining overhead, casting deep shadows on the forest floor. Mara felt a chill run down her spine, an instinctual response to the oppressive atmosphere.

The trail led her to a small clearing, and there she found the source of the blood - a deer, its body torn and lifeless. The scene was gruesome, but it provided some answers. The blood on the trees was likely the result of a predator dragging its prey through the forest.

But as Mara examined the scene, something didn't add up. The deer's wounds were too precise, too clean to be the work of a typical forest predator. And there was something else - a faint symbol etched into the ground near the deer, almost hidden beneath the fallen leaves.

Mara took photos of the symbol, a sense of unease growing within her. This was more than a simple animal attack. There was a deliberate aspect to it, a ritualistic quality that couldn't be ignored.

She reported her findings, requesting backup and a wildlife expert to examine the scene. As she waited, Mara couldn't shake the feeling that she was being watched. The forest seemed to be holding its breath, waiting for her next move.

When the experts arrived, they confirmed her suspicions. The deer's wounds were not consistent with any known predator in the area. And the symbol? It matched no known natural or cultural markings.

As the sun began to set, casting long shadows across the clearing, Mara knew that this case was just beginning. The blood on the bark was a clue to something much deeper, a mystery that was woven into the very heart of Blackwood Forest.

She left the forest as night began to fall, but the case stayed with her, haunting her thoughts. Blackwood Forest was a place of beauty, but beneath its green canopy lay secrets, dark and waiting. The blood on the bark was just the beginning, a doorway into a case that would challenge everything Mara knew about the natural world.

13

Chapter 13: Forbidden Footsteps

The sky was a tapestry of stars above Blackwood Forest, a sight seldom seen by those who feared the forest's nocturnal mysteries. Ethan, a local college student with a fascination for the forbidden, was drawn to the legends of an off-limits area deep within the woods. Despite warnings and rumors, he was determined to uncover the truth behind the so-called 'Forbidden Footsteps'—a path said to lead to places unknown and filled with danger.

His journey began at the edge of the forest, where the last vestiges of the town's lights faded into the darkness. Equipped with a flashlight, a map, and a rebellious spirit, Ethan ventured into the heart of Blackwood. The forest at night was a different realm, each sound amplified, each shadow a hiding place for imagined terrors.

He moved with purpose, following an old, forgotten trail he had uncovered in his research. The path was overgrown, barely visible, and every step seemed to reinforce the feeling that he was treading where he shouldn't. The Forbidden Footsteps were not just a physical path, but a boundary of the unknown.

As he delved deeper, Ethan noticed something unsettling. The forest was eerily quiet, devoid of the nocturnal chorus that usually filled the air. It was as if the wildlife knew to stay away from this part of the woods. He pressed on, driven by a mix of curiosity and bravado.

The path led to a narrow ravine, its sides steep and treacherous. Here, the Forbidden Footsteps became more pronounced, etched into the very earth as if countless others had walked this path before him. Ethan felt a chill run down his spine. The legends spoke of this place as a threshold to something ancient and powerful.

He descended carefully into the ravine. The air grew colder, the atmosphere heavier. It was as though he was moving into the bowels of the earth itself. At the bottom, the path continued, leading into a dense thicket that seemed to absorb his flashlight's beam.

Ethan pushed through the thicket and found himself in a clearing, but it was unlike any he had seen before. The ground was covered in a fine, white ash, and in the center stood an ancient stone altar, its surface marked with symbols that seemed to dance in the dim light.

He approached the altar, his heart pounding in his chest. The symbols were a language he couldn't understand, but they emanated a power that was almost tangible. Ethan reached out to touch the stone, and as he did, the ground trembled beneath him.

A low rumble filled the air, growing louder, as if something was awakening. Ethan stumbled back, his mind racing. He had heard stories of guardians and spirits that watched over certain places in the forest, but he had dismissed them as mere tales.

Now, as the air around him vibrated with a force he could neither see nor understand, he realized he had trespassed into a realm that was not meant for the living. The Forbidden Footsteps were forbidden for a reason.

He turned to leave, but the path he had come through was gone, replaced by a dense wall of vegetation. Panic set in as he realized he was lost, the forest closing in on him. The rumbling ceased, replaced by a deafening silence.

Ethan wandered through the night, each turn leading him further into the labyrinth of the forest. It was only by the grace of the morning light, filtering through the canopy, that he found his way back to the familiar paths of Blackwood.

Exhausted, scared, but alive, Ethan emerged from the forest a changed person. The Forbidden Footsteps had shown him that some legends were based in truth, and some boundaries were not meant to be crossed.

His adventure into the depths of Blackwood Forest had revealed a world that existed alongside his own, a world of ancient powers and unspoken rules. The Forbidden Footsteps were a reminder that some mysteries of the forest were best left unexplored.

14

Chapter 14: The Chilling Mist

As twilight descended upon Blackwood Forest, a dense, chilling mist began to rise from the damp earth, enveloping the trees in a ghostly shroud. Clara, a local meteorologist and environmentalist, was intrigued by this phenomenon, which seemed to occur only within a specific area of the forest. Known for her scientific curiosity, Clara set out to study this mysterious mist, seeking to understand its origins and properties.

Equipped with her weather instruments and environmental sensors, Clara ventured into the forest just as the evening light began to wane. The forest, usually alive with the sounds of nocturnal creatures, was eerily silent, the stillness amplified by the thickening mist.

As she progressed deeper into the forest, Clara noted how the temperature dropped significantly within the mist, far more than what was usual for this time of the evening. Her instruments confirmed the sudden change, showing readings that defied normal meteorological patterns.

The mist seemed to have a life of its own, swirling and moving in patterns that suggested an unseen force at work. Clara followed it, fascinated by its behavior. The mist led her to a secluded part of the forest, a place she hadn't explored before.

Here, the trees were older, their gnarled branches intertwining in a complex canopy above. The mist was denser, reducing visibility to a few feet. Clara felt a shiver run down her spine, not just from the cold, but from the realization that this place was different, almost otherworldly.

As she set up her equipment to take more readings, Clara noticed something strange—despite the mist, there was no dew on the ground or on the leaves. It was as if the mist existed independently of the normal condensation process. She collected samples of the mist using specialized containers, hoping to analyze its composition back in her lab.

While engrossed in her work, Clara heard a soft, melodic sound, like a whisper carried on the wind. She turned, trying to locate the source, but the mist made it impossible to see. The sound seemed to surround her, a haunting melody that was both beautiful and unsettling.

Compelled by the sound, Clara ventured further into the mist. The melody grew louder, a symphonic chorus that resonated through the trees. Then, as suddenly as it had appeared, the mist began to dissipate, revealing a hidden grove bathed in moonlight.

In the center of the grove stood an ancient stone monument, its surface covered in intricate carvings. The melody seemed to emanate from the stone, a song older than time itself. Clara approached, her scientific mind struggling to make sense of the phenomenon.

The stone was cold to the touch, but the air around it vibrated with energy. Clara's instruments registered off the charts, indicating electromagnetic fields far beyond what she had ever recorded. The melody reached a crescendo, filling the grove with a sound that seemed to speak directly to her soul.

Then, as abruptly as it had begun, the melody ceased, and the mist returned, enveloping the grove and the stone monument once again. Clara found herself standing in silence, the moonlight fading as the mist obscured the sky.

She gathered her equipment and samples, her mind racing with questions and theories. The Chilling Mist of Blackwood Forest was more than just a meteorological anomaly; it was a gateway to something ancient and unknown.

As Clara made her way back through the forest, the mist slowly receding with the approaching dawn, she knew that her findings would challenge the boundaries of science and nature. The Chilling Mist was a mystery that beckoned to be solved, a phenomenon that blurred the line between the natural and the supernatural.

15

❧

Chapter 15: Cabin of Whispers

The night was moonless and dark, the kind of darkness that seemed to consume all light, deep in the heart of Blackwood Forest. Amidst this impenetrable darkness stood a cabin, old and dilapidated, its history lost to time. Known among the locals as the Cabin of Whispers, it was a place shrouded in tales and rumors, a place many dared not approach. But for Avery, a young and bold paranormal investigator, this cabin was an irresistible enigma.

Avery had always been captivated by the unexplained, and the Cabin of Whispers, with its reputation for mysterious voices and unexplained phenomena, was a puzzle she was determined to solve. Equipped with her recording devices, EMF meters, and a healthy dose of skepticism, she approached the cabin under the cloak of night, the ideal time for any paranormal investigation.

The forest around the cabin was unusually quiet, as if the wildlife instinctively avoided the area. Avery's footsteps seemed unnaturally loud as she walked up to the cabin, the wood creaking under her weight. The structure was old, the wood rotting in places, the windows broken and empty, like hollow eyes watching her approach.

As she stepped inside, a chill ran through her. The air inside was stale and cold, and a sense of unease immediately washed over her. The cabin was sparsely furnished, with remnants of its past scattered around – a rusted bed frame, a broken table, and an old fireplace, long cold.

Avery set up her equipment, her EMF meters strategically placed around the cabin. She began recording, asking questions into the silence, hoping for a response from whatever might be lingering in the cabin.

For a long time, there was nothing but the sound of her own breathing and the occasional groan of the settling cabin. But then, Avery heard it – a faint whisper, almost inaudible, coming from the corner of the room. She turned her recorder in the direction of the sound, holding her breath.

The whisper grew louder, a soft, undulating voice speaking in a language she couldn't understand. The words were foreign, ancient, and yet they carried an emotional depth that transcended language. Avery felt a mix of fear and fascination – this was what she had come for, but now that it was happening, it felt overwhelming.

As she listened, the temperature in the room dropped, her breath visible in the cold air. The whispers seemed to be coming from all around her now, a chorus of voices speaking in unison. Avery's EMF meters lit up, indicating a presence, an energy that couldn't be explained.

Then, as suddenly as it had begun, the whispering stopped. The temperature returned to normal, and the EMF meters went silent. Avery stood in the quiet cabin, her mind racing to process what she had just experienced.

She collected her equipment, her recordings now holding what could be vital evidence of the paranormal. As she left the cabin, Avery looked back, the moonlight casting eerie shadows across the clearing. The Cabin of Whispers had lived up to its name, offering more questions than answers.

Back in her makeshift lab, Avery analyzed the recordings, the whisperings still clear and haunting. They were a mystery wrapped in an enigma, a voice from the past reaching out through the veil of time.

The investigation into the Cabin of Whispers had only just begun, but Avery knew she had touched something profound, something that challenged her understanding of the world. The cabin, nestled deep in Blackwood Forest, was more than just an old structure; it was a keeper of secrets, a whispering entity that spoke of lost histories and hidden truths.

16

In the dense, shadowy heart of Blackwood Forest, a deep, unsettling growl reverberated through the trees, disturbing the usual tranquility of the night. This sound, neither animal nor human, had been reported by several hikers and campers over the past weeks, stirring both fear and curiosity in the local community. Among those drawn to this mystery was Liam, a wildlife biologist and amateur cryptozoologist, eager to identify the source of this unearthly growl.

Equipped with audio recording gear, night vision goggles, and an array of wildlife tracking tools, Liam ventured into the forest as twilight faded into night. The forest, a mosaic of shadows and whispers under the moonlight, seemed to throb with an unseen life. Liam's heart raced with a mixture of excitement and apprehension. He was well-versed in the sounds of the forest, but this growl was something entirely different, something primal and unknown.

As he trekked deeper into the woods, the familiar sounds of

nocturnal creatures filled the air, but they were underscored by a palpable tension, as if the forest itself was holding its breath. Liam checked his equipment, ensuring his recording devices were primed to capture any unusual sounds.

Suddenly, the growl echoed through the trees, closer and more menacing than before. It was a deep, resonant sound that seemed to vibrate through the very ground beneath his feet. Liam felt a chill run down his spine. The growl was unlike any animal he knew – it was as if the forest itself had found a voice, ancient and ominous.

Guided by the direction of the sound, Liam moved cautiously, his senses heightened. The growl continued, intermittent but always nearby, leading him further into the forest. He noticed something peculiar – the wildlife seemed to quieten in the wake of the sound, creating pockets of eerie silence.

As he approached a small clearing, the growl sounded again, so close that it seemed to be right at the edge of the trees. Liam readied his equipment, his hands steady despite his racing heart. He scanned the clearing with his night vision goggles, but the source of the sound remained elusive, hidden in the dark embrace of the forest.

Liam decided to set up a makeshift observation post. He positioned his audio equipment to capture the growl from different angles, hoping to triangulate its source. Hours passed, the growl occurring at irregular intervals, each time as inexplicable as the last.

Then, in the early hours of the morning, the growl ceased abruptly. The forest fell into a deep silence, the kind that feels like a held breath. Liam waited, but the sound did not return. As dawn broke, painting the forest in hues of gold and green, he packed up his equipment, the recordings secured and unharmed.

Back in his lab, Liam analyzed the audio, but the more he listened, the more perplexing the growl became. It matched no known wildlife species, and its acoustic properties were unlike anything he had encountered. The growl seemed to exist outside the known natural spectrum, raising questions that defied easy answers.

Word of Liam's investigation spread, attracting the interest of both the scientific community and the public. Theories abounded – an undiscovered animal species, a geological phenomenon, or something more mystical, tied to the ancient lore of Blackwood Forest.

For Liam, the investigation into the unearthly growl became a personal obsession. He returned to the forest night after night, collecting more data, seeking patterns or clues that could shed light on this mystery. The growl, however, remained an enigma, a voice in the darkness that echoed with the mysteries of Blackwood Forest.

The Unearthly Growl of Blackwood became a legend in its own right, a tantalizing mystery that continued to beckon the brave and the curious. For Liam, it was a reminder of the vast unknowns that still existed in the natural world, a call from the wild that defied understanding, as elusive and haunting as the forest from which it emanated.

17

∽

Chapter 17: Nightmares at Dawn

The first light of dawn had just begun to pierce the dense canopy of Blackwood Forest, casting long, eerie shadows among the trees. This was the time when the night's fears were supposed to fade with the darkness, but for Jenna, a local artist who had spent the night in the forest for inspiration, the nightmares were just beginning.

Jenna, known for her vivid and often unsettling landscapes, had ventured into Blackwood Forest to capture its nocturnal essence. She had always found something captivating about the forest at night, its shadows and sounds painting a picture of mystery and wonder. But this night had been different. As she packed up her canvas and paints, her hands still trembled from the dreams that had plagued her as she slept under the forest's watchful eye.

Her dreams had been vivid and chaotic, filled with twisted visions of the forest. In her nightmares, the trees had come alive, their branches reaching for her, their roots twisting and turning into grotesque shapes. She had heard voices in the wind, calling her name, their tones both enticing and menacing.

Jenna shook her head, trying to dispel the remnants of the dreams. She had always believed in the power of dreams to inspire, but these had left her with a feeling of unease, a sense that she had glimpsed something forbidden.

As she made her way back through the forest, the first rays of dawn casting light on her path, she noticed something odd. Her surroundings seemed subtly changed. The trees looked different, their shapes more sinister, mirroring the twisted forms of her nightmares. The forest, which she had walked through so many times, now felt unfamiliar, as if it had revealed a hidden face.

Jenna's pace quickened, an instinctual desire to leave the forest growing with every step. She could not shake the feeling of being watched, of eyes following her movements through the trees. The whispers of the wind seemed to carry echoes of her dreams, blurring the lines between sleep and wakefulness.

As she neared the edge of the forest, Jenna stopped in her tracks. There, on the path ahead of her, were footprints. But these were not human or animal; they were strange, distorted impressions that matched the unearthly beings from her dreams. She looked around, her heart racing, but there was no one and nothing to be seen.

The forest had fallen silent, a heavy, expectant silence that felt like a breath being held. Jenna moved quickly now, almost running, her artist's curiosity replaced by a primal need to escape.

When she finally emerged from the forest, the morning light seemed harsh, too bright. She looked back once, half-expecting to see something emerge from the trees, but there was only the forest, still and silent.

Back in her studio, Jenna's paintings took on a new, disturbing quality. Her canvases were filled with twisted trees and shadowy figures, echoes of her nightmares at dawn. The forest she had once found inspiring now held a sense of foreboding, a reminder of the night when her dreams had spilled into reality.

The experience in Blackwood Forest changed Jenna. She continued to paint, but her works now spoke of the thin veil between dream and wakefulness, of the hidden faces of nature, and of the nightmares that linger at the edge of dawn.

18

Chapter 18: The Creeping Fog

As dusk settled over Blackwood Forest, a dense, creeping fog began to roll in from the west, blanketing the woods in a thick, opaque shroud. Simon, a seasoned park ranger with years of experience in these woods, had noticed a pattern in the behavior of this peculiar fog. Unlike the typical mist that occasionally enveloped the forest, this fog seemed to move with purpose, engulfing the landscape in a ghostly embrace.

Intrigued by this anomaly, Simon had decided to investigate the phenomenon. Equipped with his weather monitoring instruments and a sturdy flashlight, he set out into the increasingly obscured forest. The fog transformed the familiar paths into a maze of shadows and silhouettes, distorting and hiding the world as Simon knew it.

As he ventured deeper, Simon noticed that the fog seemed to ebb and flow with an almost rhythmic pattern, as if it were breathing. The temperature within the fog was noticeably colder, and a fine layer of moisture coated everything it touched. His flashlight beam struggled to penetrate the fog, creating eerie patterns of light and darkness.

Simon's instruments revealed unusual fluctuations in humidity and temperature as he moved through the fog. These readings defied typical meteorological patterns, suggesting that the fog was not a natural occurrence, or at least not entirely so.

The forest was eerily silent within the fog, the usual chorus of nocturnal creatures absent. This silence was unsettling, but Simon pressed on, determined to uncover the source of this phenomenon. He made his way to a small, open meadow, a place he knew well, but under the veil of the fog, it appeared otherworldly.

As he surveyed the meadow, a sudden movement caught his eye. It was a shadowy figure, moving slowly through the fog at the edge of the clearing. Simon called out, but the figure did not respond, continuing its slow, deliberate movement. Simon followed, his curiosity piqued.

The figure led him to the heart of the forest, to an ancient, gnarled tree that Simon recognized as one of the oldest in Blackwood. The tree stood taller and more imposing than he remembered, its branches twisting into the fog.

Here, the fog seemed to originate, swirling around the tree in a mesmerizing dance. Simon approached the tree cautiously, his instruments recording off-the-chart readings. He reached out to touch the tree, and as he did, the fog suddenly thickened, enveloping him completely.

The temperature dropped sharply, and Simon felt an inexplicable sense of disorientation. When the fog finally cleared, he found himself standing in a different part of the forest, one he didn't recognize. His compass spun wildly, unable to find a bearing.

Simon realized that the fog was more than just a weather phenomenon; it was a gateway, a moving, living entity that connected different parts of the forest in ways he couldn't understand. The ancient tree seemed to be its anchor, a center of power and mystery.

After what felt like hours of wandering, Simon eventually found his way back to familiar ground. The fog had dissipated as quickly as it had appeared, leaving the forest clear and calm.

Back at the ranger station, Simon documented his experience, his mind racing with questions and theories. The Creeping Fog of Blackwood Forest was a mystery that blurred the lines between the natural and the supernatural. It was a reminder of the hidden wonders and terrors that lay within the heart of the forest, moving and breathing in ways that defied explanation.

19

Chapter 19: Sinister Whispers

The night was unusually still in the heart of Blackwood Forest. A thin sliver of a crescent moon barely illuminated the dense canopy of trees, casting ghostly shadows on the forest floor. It was in this haunting setting that Elise, an aspiring novelist with a penchant for horror and mystery, found herself drawn to the forest's most enigmatic and feared spot, known as the Whispering Hollow.

Rumors and tales had long circulated in the nearby town about Whispering Hollow. It was said that at night, one could hear whispers there, not of the wind or animals, but of an unknown, sinister origin. Elise, fueled by a mix of intrigue and a desire for inspiration for her next novel, ventured into the forest, her digital recorder in hand to capture any unexplained phenomena.

As she made her way through the dark, tangled underbrush, Elise felt the oppressive weight of the forest's gaze. The silence was profound, broken only by the occasional crack of a twig under her boots. Her heart pounded in her chest, not just from the hike, but from the anticipation of what she might find.

Finally, Elise arrived at the edge of Whispering Hollow. The area was a small depression in the forest floor, surrounded by ancient, gnarled trees that seemed to lean inward, as if guarding a secret. She stepped into the hollow, and immediately, a chill ran down her spine. The temperature here was noticeably colder, and the air felt thick, charged with an unspoken energy.

Elise switched on her recorder and sat down on a fallen log, her ears straining for any sound. At first, there was nothing. But as the night deepened, a faint whispering began to fill the air. It was soft, almost inaudible at first, but gradually it grew louder, a chorus of hushed, indiscernible voices.

The whispers seemed to come from all around her, the words unintelligible. Elise felt a rising sense of dread. The voices didn't seem threatening, but they carried a tone of urgency, of desperation. She stood up, her recorder still capturing the eerie symphony, and tried to locate the source of the voices.

As she moved through the hollow, the whispers seemed to follow her, growing in intensity. Elise's scientific mind struggled to find a logical explanation. Could it be the wind funneling through the hollow, or the echoes of nocturnal animals? But deep down, she knew this was different; the whispers had a human quality to them, a purpose.

Suddenly, the whispers stopped, replaced by a single, clear voice. It spoke in a language Elise couldn't understand, yet its tone was unmistakable – a warning. The air grew colder, and a dense mist began to rise from the ground, enveloping Elise.

Panicked, Elise turned to leave the hollow, but in the swirling mist, she lost her sense of direction. The voice continued, louder now, its message urgent. Elise felt an overwhelming sense of being watched, of a presence in the mist with her.

After what felt like hours, Elise finally emerged from the mist, finding herself on the familiar path leading out of the forest. The night was beginning to give way to the first light of dawn, and as she looked back at Whispering Hollow, the mist and the voices were gone, as if they had never been.

Back home, Elise listened to the recordings. The whispers were there, a haunting testament to her experience. She couldn't shake the feeling that she had touched something ancient and forbidden in Whispering Hollow, a secret that the forest had reluctantly shared.

The experience at Whispering Hollow became the inspiration for Elise's next novel, a tale of a haunted forest and the voices that lingered in its shadows. But for Elise, it was more than just a story; it was a reminder of the night she had heard the sinister whispers of Blackwood Forest, a memory that would stay with her, both haunting and inspiring her writing for years to come.

20

Chapter 20: Eerie Illuminations

The night in Blackwood Forest was alive with an otherworldly glow. Bioluminescent fungi, a rare and mesmerizing phenomenon, had illuminated a secluded section of the woods, casting an ethereal, eerie light over the underbrush. This spectacle, known to the locals as the Eerie Illuminations, had long been a subject of fascination and superstition. For Thomas, a nature photographer with a keen interest in capturing the forest's hidden wonders, this was a much-awaited event.

Armed with his camera and a sense of wonder, Thomas ventured into the forest under the cover of darkness. The bioluminescent display was said to occur only a few times a year, under specific conditions, and lasted for just a few hours. His excitement was palpable as he made his way through the forest, guided by the soft, otherworldly glow in the distance.

As he approached the site of the Eerie Illuminations, Thomas was struck by the surreal beauty of the scene. The ground was carpeted with glowing fungi, emitting a soft, blue-green light that illuminated the forest in a spectral hue. It was like stepping into a dream or a scene from a fantasy novel.

He set up his camera, capturing the luminous landscape from various angles. The light from the fungi was faint, yet it cast sharp, defined shadows, creating a landscape that was both haunting and beautiful. Thomas felt a profound sense of peace as he worked, surrounded by the gentle glow of the forest.

But as he moved deeper into the illuminated area, Thomas began to notice something unusual. Among the usual patterns of the glowing fungi, there were anomalies – shapes and symbols that seemed to form a deliberate pattern. These weren't random growths; they looked almost like a form of writing or communication, etched in light on the forest floor.

Intrigued, Thomas took several photographs of these patterns, his mind racing with questions. Were these natural occurrences, or something more? The forest had always been a place of mystery, but this discovery hinted at something deeper, something hidden in the very fabric of Blackwood.

As the night wore on, the intensity of the bioluminescence began to fade, the glowing patterns slowly disappearing with the approaching dawn. Thomas stayed until the last traces of light vanished, leaving him in the quiet, dark forest.

Back at his studio, Thomas examined the photographs, the luminous patterns even more pronounced in the captured images. He reached out to mycologists and other experts, sharing his findings, but no one could provide a clear explanation. The patterns defied scientific understanding, blurring the line between the natural and the mystical.

Word of Thomas's discovery spread, sparking interest and debate among both the scientific community and local lore enthusiasts. Some speculated that the patterns were a form of communication from the forest itself, a message or a sign. Others believed them to be remnants of an ancient, forgotten practice, perhaps related to the local legends and myths of Blackwood Forest.

For Thomas, the Eerie Illuminations became a personal obsession. He returned to the forest night after night, hoping to witness and document the phenomenon again. But the glowing patterns never reappeared, remaining a singular, unexplained event.

The photographs of the Eerie Illuminations took on a life of their own, becoming a subject of fascination and mystery. For Thomas, they were a reminder of the forest's hidden depths, a testament to the wonders and mysteries that lay waiting in the shadows of Blackwood Forest. The glowing patterns, captured in his photographs, stood as a tantalizing enigma, an unsolved riddle in the heart of the forest.

21

Chapter 21: The Claw Marks

The morning sun filtered through the dense canopy of Blackwood Forest, casting a dappled light on the forest floor. Detective Sarah Bennett walked along a narrow, winding path, her eyes trained on the ground. She was here to investigate a series of mysterious claw marks that had appeared on several trees deep within the forest.

As a detective with a background in environmental science, Sarah had seen her fair share of animal attacks and natural phenomena. But the reports about these claw marks were different – they were larger and more deliberate than any animal she knew of in the region.

Arriving at the first marked tree, Sarah observed the claw marks closely. They were deep and evenly spaced, running vertically down the trunk. Each mark was several inches long and appeared to have been made with significant force. The markings were fresh, suggesting that whatever made them had passed through the area recently.

Intrigued, Sarah took out her camera and notepad, documenting the size, shape, and pattern of the claw marks. She moved from tree to tree, finding similar markings on several others. The marks were consistent – always the same size and depth, as if made by the same creature.

As she ventured deeper into the forest, Sarah noticed an unsettling silence. The usual sounds of birds and small animals were absent, as if the entire forest was holding its breath. She felt a growing sense of unease, the hairs on the back of her neck standing up.

The trail of claw marks led Sarah to a small clearing, where she found something that made her pause. In the center of the clearing was a large, uprooted tree, its roots exposed, creating a natural barrier. And on this tree were claw marks unlike the others – they were larger, more chaotic, as if made in a frenzy.

Sarah examined the uprooted tree, her mind racing with theories. Was this the den of whatever creature made the marks? Or the site of a struggle? She took several photographs, her detective instincts telling her that this was a significant piece of the puzzle.

As she circled the tree, Sarah discovered something else – a piece of fabric torn and caught on the rough bark. It was a piece of clothing, human-made, suggesting that whatever happened here involved a person. This discovery shifted the nature of her investigation, hinting at a possible missing person or an unreported attack.

Sarah decided to widen her search area, looking for more clues. As she moved through the forest, she noticed more signs of disturbance – broken branches, disturbed underbrush, and more claw marks, each set leading further into the forest.

Her search brought her to a steep ravine, the sides covered in dense foliage. It was here that Sarah found the most disturbing evidence yet. At the bottom of the ravine, partially hidden by the underbrush, was a body.

Calling for backup, Sarah carefully made her way down into the ravine. The body was that of a man, his clothes torn in several places. The injuries were severe, consistent with an animal attack, but there was something unnatural about them. The claw marks on his body were the same as those on the trees – large, deep, and deliberate.

As Sarah waited for the forensic team, she pondered the mystery of the claw marks. What kind of creature could make such marks? And why were they found on both trees and a human victim?

The investigation into the claw marks of Blackwood Forest became a top priority. The local wildlife agencies were consulted, camera traps were set up, and the forest was searched for any signs of an unknown predator.

But the mystery remained unsolved. The claw marks did not match any known wildlife in the area, and no further evidence was found despite extensive searches. The forest seemed to have swallowed up any answers, leaving only questions and theories.

For Detective Sarah Bennett, the case of the claw marks in Blackwood Forest remained open, a haunting reminder of the mysteries hidden in the heart of the woods. The claw marks, both on the trees and the unfortunate victim, stood as a chilling testament to the unknown dangers lurking in the shadows of the forest.

22

Chapter 22: Terror in the Thicket

The dense thicket of Blackwood Forest was notorious among the locals for its impenetrable undergrowth and the sense of foreboding it evoked. It was here, in this uninviting part of the woods, that a series of unexplained disappearances had recently occurred. As the head of the local search and rescue team, Emily Donovan was determined to uncover the truth behind these incidents.

The day was overcast, the heavy clouds casting a somber mood over the forest. Emily, along with her trained search team and a couple of police dogs, began their expedition into the heart of the thicket. The undergrowth was thick, a tangled maze of brambles and overhanging branches that made progress slow and treacherous.

As they delved deeper, Emily couldn't shake off the feeling of being watched. The thicket had a reputation for being a place where the line between legend and reality blurred. Whispered tales of a shadowy presence lurking in the dense foliage were common in the town, stories she had dismissed until now.

The dogs, usually energetic and noisy, moved with uncharacteristic hesitance, their ears perked up, sensing something unseen. The team communicated in hushed tones, their voices barely rising above the rustling leaves.

Suddenly, one of the dogs began to bark furiously, its body tense and alert. Emily and her team hurried over, finding a small clearing they hadn't known existed. In the center of the clearing was a dilapidated structure, half-consumed by the forest. It looked like an old shack, its wood rotten and covered in moss.

The dog was barking at the entrance of the shack, its nose pressed to the ground. Emily approached cautiously, her hand resting on the pistol at her belt. She signaled for two team members to flank her as she stepped inside.

The interior was dark and damp, the air stale. The floorboards creaked under their weight. In the corner of the room, they found a backpack and a camera – belongings of one of the missing persons. The camera's memory card was still intact.

As they searched the shack, a sudden, loud crack echoed from outside, like the breaking of a large branch. The team rushed out, only to find nothing amiss. But the atmosphere had changed; the forest seemed to close in around them, the shadows lengthening and deepening.

The decision was made to retreat and analyze the camera's contents back at headquarters. As they made their way out of the thicket, Emily couldn't shake the feeling of relief, as if they were being allowed to leave, rather than simply finding their way out.

Back at headquarters, the camera revealed its secrets. The photos were mostly of the forest, but the last few images were disturbing. They showed the shack, but with a shadowy figure standing in the doorway, its features indistinct but unmistakably menacing.

The discovery sent a chill down Emily's spine. The figure matched descriptions from old tales of the forest – a guardian of sorts, a presence that kept intruders at bay.

The case of the terror in the thicket remained unresolved. The forest kept its secrets, and the shack stood silent and watchful. Emily knew that the thicket was more than just a dense cluster of trees; it was a place where the unknown reigned, a reminder of the mysteries that lay hidden in the shadows of Blackwood Forest.

23

Chapter 23: The Ancient Oak

In the heart of Blackwood Forest stood an oak tree of colossal size, its branches sprawling wide, its trunk thick and gnarled with age. Known as the Ancient Oak, it was a living testament to the forest's history, believed to be over a thousand years old. Local legend held that the tree possessed an otherworldly wisdom and that those who listened closely might hear its whispers. This legend had always fascinated Dr. Lydia Marsh, a dendrologist dedicated to the study of ancient trees.

Armed with her scientific instruments and a deeply ingrained respect for the forest, Lydia set out to study the Ancient Oak. Her goal was to unlock the secrets it held in its rings, hoping to gain insight into the climatic changes and events it had witnessed over the centuries.

The journey to the Ancient Oak was a familiar one for Lydia. She had visited the tree many times, each visit deepening her awe for its majesty and significance. As she approached, the forest seemed to open up, the smaller trees bowing away from the oak as if in reverence.

Lydia began her work, carefully taking measurements and samples, all the while speaking softly to the tree, as was her habit. She believed that a connection with nature was essential to understanding it. Her instruments gathered data, but Lydia knew that the true essence of the Ancient Oak lay beyond numbers and figures.

As dusk approached, Lydia decided to camp near the tree, as she had done on previous occasions. The night in Blackwood Forest was a symphony of sounds, but around the Ancient Oak, a serene quiet prevailed, as if the forest itself was pausing to pay homage.

Lydia sat with her back against the tree, her eyes closed, breathing in the earthy scent of the forest. It was then that she noticed it – a faint humming sound, almost like a whisper. It seemed to be emanating from the tree itself. Lydia listened intently, a chill running down her spine. The sound was melodic, rising and falling in a rhythm that felt ancient and meaningful.

She reached out, placing her hands on the rugged bark of the Ancient Oak, and the humming grew louder, more distinct. It was as if the tree was communicating, its vibrations telling a story of centuries past, of the life it had witnessed, the storms it had weathered, and the countless seasons it had seen change.

Lydia stayed like that for hours, immersed in the experience, her scientific mind grappling with the inexplicable nature of the sound. Was it the wind, playing tricks as it passed through the branches, or was there something more, something mystical about the Ancient Oak?

Morning light broke through the canopy, casting dappled patterns on the forest floor. Lydia packed up her equipment, her mind still reeling from the night's experience. She knew that her data would contribute valuable information to the scientific community, but the true mystery of the Ancient Oak, its whispers, remained unsolved.

Back in her lab, Lydia analyzed the samples and data, but her thoughts kept drifting back to the humming sound, the whispers of the Ancient Oak. It was a reminder that some aspects of nature defy scientific explanation, that there are mysteries in the natural world that remain beyond our understanding.

For Lydia, the Ancient Oak of Blackwood Forest remained a symbol of the enduring mystery and majesty of nature, a guardian of history, whispering its ancient tales to those who would listen.

24

Chapter 24: Murmurs of the Past

In the twilight hours of a cool autumn evening, historian and folklore enthusiast Jacob Edwards trekked through the underbrush of Blackwood Forest. His destination was the remains of an old settlement rumored to be hidden within the forest, a place that locals referred to as the "Ghost Town." As someone deeply fascinated by the intertwining of history and legend, Jacob sought to uncover the stories and murmurs of the past that this forgotten town whispered.

The path to the settlement was overgrown and barely visible, a faint trail winding through the dense foliage. Jacob moved carefully, his flashlight casting eerie shadows among the trees. The forest was alive with the sounds of nocturnal creatures, but there was an underlying silence, a stillness that spoke of abandonment and decay.

After an hour of navigating the thick woods, Jacob arrived at the outskirts of the old settlement. The first structures that greeted him were dilapidated wooden houses, their roofs caved in, their walls covered in moss and ivy. The settlement had been abandoned for decades, maybe even a century, and nature had reclaimed much of it.

Jacob's heart raced with excitement as he walked through the ghost town, his flashlight illuminating the remnants of a bygone era. He could see the remains of a well in the town square, a rusted-out carriage half-buried under fallen leaves, and a weathered statue of the town's founder.

As he explored, Jacob took notes and photographs, documenting his findings. He was particularly drawn to an old church at the far end of the town. Its structure was more intact than the others, its wooden doors hanging off their hinges. Inside, the pews were coated in dust, and an old bible lay open on the pulpit, its pages yellowed with age.

Jacob felt a profound sense of connection to the past in this place. He could almost hear the murmurs of the townsfolk who once lived here, their joys and sorrows, their dreams and fears. He imagined them gathering in this very church, their voices echoing off the walls.

As night deep, Jacob decided to camp within the church, feeling a sense of safety within its walls. He set up his tent and sleeping bag, then sat outside, looking up at the stars through the clearing in the trees.

That night, Jacob experienced a series of vivid dreams. He dreamt of the town in its heyday – the sound of children playing in the streets, the smell of food cooking in homes, the tolling of the church bell. He saw faces, heard laughter, and felt the bustling energy of life.

When he awoke the next morning, Jacob wondered if the dreams had been a product of his imagination or if the town had somehow shared its memories with him. The experience was both surreal and enlightening, blurring the lines between history and the supernatural.

Packing up his gear, Jacob took one last look at the church and the ghost town. He felt a sense of gratitude for the stories and memories he had uncovered, a deeper understanding of the people who had once called this place home.

Back in the modern world, Jacob shared his findings and experiences, his story adding another layer to the rich tapestry of Blackwood Forest's history. The Ghost Town, with its murmurs of the past, remained a hidden jewel in the forest, a poignant reminder of the transient nature of life and the enduring power of memory.

25

Chapter 25: The Enigma of Blackwood

In the heart of Blackwood Forest, amidst the intertwining branches and ancient stones, lay secrets as old as time. Dr. Helena Barrett, an anthropologist and mythologist, had dedicated her life to unraveling these mysteries. Her latest project, aptly titled "The Enigma of Blackwood," aimed to piece together the forest's history through its folklore, archaeological evidence, and natural phenomena.

Helena's journey into the depths of Blackwood was more than just academic; it was a personal quest. She believed that the forest held keys to understanding not only the past of the region but also broader insights into human belief and nature's mysteries.

Armed with her research equipment, journals, and a keen sense of observation, Helena embarked on her exploration. Blackwood Forest was a labyrinth of natural beauty and mystery, its dense canopy casting ever-changing shadows on the forest floor. Every tree, rock, and stream seemed to hold a story, a piece of the puzzle she was determined to solve.

Her first stop was the ancient standing stones located in the deeper part of the forest. Arranged in a circle, with inscriptions long worn away by time, these stones were a tangible connection to the past. Helena set up her instruments to measure their alignment and composition, hypothesizing they were part of a larger ritualistic structure used by ancient peoples.

As the days passed, Helena ventured deeper into the forest, mapping out old, forgotten paths and documenting her findings. She came across carvings on trees that were hundreds of years old, hidden clearings that seemed to have been used for gatherings, and old artifacts partially buried under layers of fallen leaves.

Each night, as she camped under the stars, Helena recorded her thoughts and theories in her journal. The forest at night was a symphony of sounds, and often, she found herself lying awake, listening to the rustling of leaves and the distant hooting of owls, wondering about the people who had walked these paths before her.

Her most significant discovery came when she found a series of cave paintings in a secluded part of the forest. These paintings depicted scenes of daily life, but also more mysterious images – figures that seemed to blend human and animal features, celestial patterns, and what appeared to be stories of interaction with supernatural entities.

These findings were a breakthrough, offering a glimpse into the belief systems and rituals of the forest's ancient inhabitants. They painted a picture of a culture deeply intertwined with the natural world, where the lines between the physical and spiritual realms were blurred.

Helena's work in Blackwood Forest continued for weeks, each day uncovering more layers of the enigma. She collaborated with other experts in history, archaeology, and ecology, piecing together a narrative of the forest's past.

However, the more she discovered, the more she realized that Blackwood Forest was a place of endless mysteries. Some of her questions were answered, but others remained, shrouded in the mists of time. The forest was a living entity, constantly changing and evolving, its secrets guarded and revealed in its own time.

"The Enigma of Blackwood" became not just a research project, but a lifelong journey for Helena. It was a quest that went beyond academic curiosity, touching on the deeper, more profound questions of humanity's connection with nature and the mysteries that lie in the heart of the wild.

Blackwood Forest remained a place of wonder and mystery, a natural tapestry woven with stories of the past, present, and perhaps even the future. For Helena and others who would follow in her footsteps, it was a reminder that some enigmas are not meant to be fully solved, but to be explored, respected, and marveled at.

26

Chapter 26: Lurking Shadows

As night descended over Blackwood Forest, a thick fog rolled in, cloaking the dense underbrush in a veil of mystery. This was the night that Tom, a local ranger with years of experience, had chosen to investigate the phenomenon known locally as the "Lurking Shadows" – strange, fleeting shapes that hikers reported seeing at the edge of their vision, especially on foggy evenings.

Tom, a pragmatic man, had always attributed these sightings to the play of light and shadow in the forest, or perhaps the overactive imaginations of city folks unaccustomed to the woods. However, the increasing frequency of these reports had piqued his curiosity. Armed with a powerful flashlight and a healthy dose of skepticism, he ventured into the heart of the forest.

The fog made the familiar paths of Blackwood appear otherworldly. Tom's flashlight beam seemed to be swallowed by the mist, its light diffusing into eerie, glowing orbs. The usual chorus of nocturnal animals was muted, and the silence was profound, broken only by the occasional drip of condensation from the tree branches.

As he walked, Tom kept his eyes peeled for any unusual movement. At first, there was nothing but the mist and the darkness. But as he ventured deeper, he began to notice fleeting movements at the periphery of his vision – quick, shadowy figures that vanished when he turned to look directly at them.

At first, Tom dismissed these as tricks of the light or shadows cast by the fog. But as he continued, the sightings became more frequent, more distinct. He could now make out humanoid shapes, darting between the trees, always just out of direct sight. A chill ran down his spine – this was unlike anything he had experienced in his years patrolling the forest.

Determined to get to the bottom of the mystery, Tom followed the shadows deeper into the forest. The terrain grew rougher, and he found himself in a part of Blackwood he didn't recognize. The fog here was thicker, the atmosphere heavier.

Then, in a small clearing, the source of the shadows revealed itself. Tom's flashlight illuminated a group of deer, their eyes reflecting the light eerily. Relief washed over him – the "lurking shadows" were just animals, their forms distorted by the fog and the darkness.

But as he observed the deer, Tom noticed something unsettling. The animals were unnaturally still, their gaze fixed on something behind him. Slowly, Tom turned around.

There, emerging from the fog, was a figure. It was tall and slender, its form vaguely human but with elongated limbs and an indistinct face. Tom froze, his rational mind struggling to process what he was seeing.

The figure stood motionless, then slowly dissipated into the fog, leaving Tom alone in the clearing. The deer, seemingly released from their trance, quickly scattered.

Tom stood there for a long time, trying to make sense of what he had seen. Had it been a trick of the light, an optical illusion created by the fog? Or had he witnessed something truly unexplainable?

Eventually, Tom made his way back to the ranger station, his mind racing with questions. The incident in the forest had shaken his skepticism. The "Lurking Shadows" of Blackwood were no longer just tales to him; they were part of the enigma that shrouded the forest – a mystery that defied explanation and reminded him of the vast, unknown depths of the natural world.

From that night on, Tom regarded the forest with a new sense of respect and wonder. Blackwood was more than just a wilderness; it was a place where the boundaries between reality and legend blurred, where the shadows held secrets yet to be understood.

27

Chapter 27: The Beckoning Hollow

The Beckoning Hollow was a place of legend in Blackwood Forest, spoken of in hushed tones by the locals. It was said to be a depression in the earth, hidden away in the densest part of the forest, where the trees grew so close together they blocked out the sky. Many tales surrounded the hollow, ranging from stories of it being a meeting place for spirits, to it being a gateway to another realm. It was these tales that drew Dr. Lisa Raymond, a cultural anthropologist, to explore this enigmatic site.

Equipped with her camera, voice recorder, and a healthy dose of skepticism, Lisa set off into the heart of Blackwood. Her aim was to document the hollow and examine any evidence of it being a site of cultural or historical significance.

The journey to the hollow was arduous. The forest seemed to thicken the closer she got to her destination, the canopy overhead forming a dark, impenetrable barrier against the sunlight. The air grew cooler, and a silence descended, the usual sounds of wildlife noticeably absent.

As Lisa made her way through the underbrush, she felt an increasing sense of unease. It was as if the forest itself was aware of her presence, the trees whispering secrets she couldn't quite grasp. She shook off the feeling, attributing it to the isolation and the eerie nature of her surroundings.

Finally, Lisa arrived at the Beckoning Hollow. It was exactly as described in the local tales – a natural amphitheater of sorts, surrounded by towering trees and dense underbrush. The ground dipped down into a shallow basin, and in the center, a large, flat stone lay embedded in the earth.

Lisa began her examination, taking photographs and making notes. The stone was covered in markings, worn and faded with age. They appeared to be some form of ancient script or symbols, possibly indicating that the hollow had been a place of significance.

As she studied the markings, Lisa began to feel a strange sensation, as if she were being watched. She turned around, half expecting to see someone, but there was no one there. Just the trees, their branches swaying gently in a non-existent breeze.

The atmosphere in the hollow began to change. A mist started to form, swirling around Lisa, growing thicker by the minute. She checked her watch and was surprised to see that hours had passed since she entered the hollow. It felt like only minutes.

Panic set in as the mist grew so dense that Lisa could barely see her hand in front of her face. She tried to find her way back, but the forest seemed to have shifted, the familiar path gone. It was as if the hollow was reshaping itself, keeping her trapped.

Then, as suddenly as it had appeared, the mist cleared, and Lisa found herself standing at the edge of the hollow, the forest around her just as she remembered it. She quickly made her way back to the safety of her camp, the hollow and its stone disappearing behind her.

Back in her camp, Lisa reviewed her photographs and recordings. The images she had taken of the stone were blurry and indistinct, and the voice recordings were filled with static. It was as if the hollow refused to be documented.

Lisa left Blackwood Forest with more questions than answers. The Beckoning Hollow remained an enigma, a place shrouded in mystery and legend. It was a reminder that some places defy explanation, existing at the fringes of our understanding, beckoning with their secrets and shadows.

28

∽

Chapter 28: Descent into Madness

In the heart of Blackwood Forest stood a hill known as Raven's Crest, a place infamous among locals for its unsettling atmosphere and bizarre occurrences. Over the years, Raven's Crest had been the site of numerous accounts of strange visions, inexplicable noises, and an overwhelming sense of dread. These phenomena had piqued the interest of Dr. Richard Harrow, a psychologist with a focus on environmental influences on mental health.

Driven by a blend of professional curiosity and personal intrigue, Richard embarked on a journey to Raven's Crest to conduct an observational study. His goal was to determine whether the environment could induce psychological disturbances or if there was a more supernatural explanation at play.

As he began his ascent up the hill, Richard noticed a subtle shift in the atmosphere. The air grew colder, and a dense fog began to roll in, obscuring his path and distorting the shapes of the trees. He pressed on, his recorder in hand, documenting his observations and feelings.

The higher Richard climbed, the more intense the sensations became. He started to hear whispers carried on the wind, indecipherable but unmistakably human. Shadows seemed to move at the corner of his vision, disappearing when he tried to focus on them. He reminded himself that these were likely tricks of the mind, influenced by the eerie setting and his own expectations.

However, as he neared the summit of Raven's Crest, Richard's rational explanations began to falter. The whispers grew louder, turning into voices calling out to him, some in anger, others in sorrow. He began to see figures in the fog, shapes that were human in form but grotesque and distorted.

Richard's heart raced as he realized he could no longer tell if he was experiencing hallucinations or a reality that defied understanding. He tried to use his psychological training to ground himself, but the voices and visions were relentless, overwhelming his senses.

In a moment of clarity, Richard decided to retreat, fearing for his mental well-being. As he descended the hill, the fog began to lift, and the voices and visions faded. By the time he reached the base of Raven's Crest, the forest had returned to normal, the oppressive atmosphere gone.

Back in his office, Richard reviewed the recordings he had made. They were a jumble of panicked breathing, rustling leaves, and fragmented mutterings. There was no evidence of the voices or visions he had experienced.

The experience at Raven's Crest deeply affected Richard. He was left questioning the boundaries between psychological phenomena and supernatural occurrences. His descent into madness, whether real or imagined, had shown him that there were aspects of the human mind and the world that were still not fully understood.

Raven's Crest remained a mystery, a place where the mind seemed to fray at the edges, blurring the line between sanity and madness. For Richard, it was a reminder of the fragility of the human psyche and the enigmatic powers that lurk in the unseen corners of the world.

∽

Chapter 29: The Final Confrontation

The night was dark and stormy, with lightning illuminating the dense canopy of Blackwood Forest in brief, stark flashes. Detective Laura Bishop, having been on the trail of a mysterious and elusive figure known only as "The Phantom of Blackwood," found herself at the heart of the forest, where all clues pointed to the final confrontation.

Over the past months, The Phantom had been linked to a series of bizarre and unexplainable events in the forest – disappearances, strange symbols found carved in trees, and eerie, untraceable sounds that echoed in the night. Laura, with her keen investigative skills and unwavering determination, had pieced together the puzzle, leading her to this decisive moment.

Armed with nothing but her flashlight and revolver, Laura ventured deeper into the forest. The storm overhead roared, the wind howling through the trees, creating a cacophony of natural chaos that masked all other sounds. She was acutely aware of the danger, the feeling of being watched growing stronger with each step.

As she reached a clearing known as the Elders' Circle, a place of ancient trees that formed a near-perfect ring, Laura saw him – The Phantom. He stood in the center of the circle, a silhouette against the sporadic lightning, his identity obscured by a hooded cloak.

Laura stepped into the circle, her revolver drawn. "It's over," she called out over the storm. "You need to come with me. Now!"

The Phantom's response was a low, chilling laugh that seemed to resonate with the very air of the forest. "You don't understand, Detective," he said, his voice deep and distorted. "This is just the beginning."

Lightning struck nearby, illuminating The Phantom's face for a split second. Laura gasped. Under the hood was not a man, but something otherworldly, its features twisted and inhuman.

The Phantom raised his hands, and the ground around the Elders' Circle began to shake. The ancient trees groaned, their branches swaying wildly as if caught in an unseen storm.

Laura realized then that The Phantom was not just a man hiding in the forest – he was part of it, a manifestation of the forest's ancient and untamed power. She understood that she could not apprehend him, not in the traditional sense. This was a force beyond human law and order.

With a sense of determination, Laura holstered her revolver. She took a step forward, her voice steady despite the fear coursing through her. "Whatever you are, whatever you want, it doesn't have to end in violence. Let's talk."

For a moment, there was silence, the storm pausing as if the forest itself was contemplating her offer. Then, The Phantom lowered his hands, and the tumultuous movement of the trees ceased. The storm abated, leaving a heavy silence in its wake.

"You are brave, Detective Bishop," The Phantom said. "But you cannot stop what is already in motion. The forest has awakened, and it will not rest until it has reclaimed what is rightfully its own."

With those cryptic words, The Phantom vanished into the night, leaving Laura alone in the Elders' Circle. She stood there for a long time, pondering his words and the future of Blackwood Forest.

The final confrontation with The Phantom had not provided the closure she had hoped for. Instead, it opened up a deeper mystery, one that intertwined the natural world with the supernatural. Laura knew that her journey with Blackwood Forest was far from over. It was a place of ancient secrets and living mysteries, a place where the line between the known and the unknown was forever blurred.